Renier-Fréduman Mundil

Uhlenspiegel with the Schilda Citizens

Uhle 1 (Volume 1)

AF209089

Renier-Fréduman Mundil

Uhlenspiegel with the Schilda Citizens

Uhle 1

Translated from German
by Hilary Teske

FSC
www.fsc.org
MIX
Papier aus ver-
antwortungsvollen
Quellen
Paper from
responsible sources
FSC® C105338

Bibliographic information from the German National Library:
The German National Library lists this publication in the
German National Bibliography; detailed bibliographic data is
available online at http://dnb.dnb.de.

Cover design: Dan Winkler
Editing: Malin Friese
Publisher: BoD · Books on Demand GmbH, Überseering 33, 22297
Hamburg, bod@bod.de Print: Libri Plureos GmbH, Friedensallee
273, 22763 Hamburg

ISBN: 978-3-8192-9930-8

For
Cameron
our sporty and mathematical
idea champion

Introduction

On sense and nonsense or on the sense of senselessness or on the sense of nonsense.

One foolishness is not good, two foolishnesses are not necessarily better, unless they try to out(trump) each other negatively or, to put it another way, they try to compensate for each other, a kind of upside-down complete compensation deal in such a way that both decompensate in the sense of not becoming even worse but disappearing together in unison.

Whether that makes sense remains to be seen. But sense is one of those things. Even in nonsense there is at least (linguistically) sense, to a certain extent the sense of not making sense, not andsense but nonsense.

Why has language never invented the word andsense? Hard to explain! Because in a common, pardon, hardly general way there are sometimes two senses in one thing. We are quite content to find one sense in a thing; at most, by using all our senses, it may be possible to elicit several senses from a thing, the sense of touch to be felt, the sense of hearing to be heard, a sense of feeling that cannot be grasped, and so on.

But all this seems senseless (or senseLess, perhaps Sense(less)).

SenseLess, the sense is perhaps a lot as in a draw, sometimes to be found in a thing, often not, just like a lot. (Translator's note: this is a play on the German word 'los' which means 'less' and 'lot in a draw' but it can't be translated directly into English).

Sense-less. That makes more sense. Someone has unhooked the sense of a thing, like you unhook a moored boat, and both sense and boat are soon gone. A boating sense, if that makes any sense. Still there but gone, just no longer there, pardon no longer here but (somewhere) still there.

So if something is sense less, pardon, senseless, that is, without sense, how can it make double sense? A nothing can hardly be doubled, something that is senseless can hardly be doubly senseless, more senseless. Senseless can only mean that the sense is no longer so solid, will soon disappear, be completely gone and haste is required to grasp it before it is even more loose, completely loose, that is, completely gone.

Senseless, that is, something without sense and in a double sense. Does that make (at least one(1)) sense? To make one out of nothing would be a magic trick, to make one out of a double sense would be an inestimable loss. A sense of loss, pardon a loss of sense.

This digression made little sense, perhaps even no sense at all.

Senseless, double sense? That makes no sense at all. Why would it make sense to look twice at something that doesn't even exist?

An empty plate doesn't get any fuller if we look at it twice. And it is absolutely senseless or absurd or even nonsensical to look twice at something that is not there. At some point, we (or our senses) will think that we have been deceived, that we (via the sometimes senseless path of our senses) have tricked ourselves, so to speak.

In a figurative sense, there is something of these thoughts in the following stories.

Two main protagonists – the lone fighter Uhlenspiegel, but with the army of his mischievous thoughts – meets the armies of the numerous Schilda citizens (rather less or let's say more neutrally armed with other thoughts).

Is such an encounter sensible? Is it perhaps senseless? Or does it perhaps make at least double sense, an and-sense, if not multiple sense?

All this remains open, just as we should go through life with open senses in order to recognize what makes sense or even to discover a hidden sense in an adventurous way - to find out where there is a (the) sense or whether it is simply missing, a kind of non-sense and in this sense as non-sense even less than nonsense, which exists somewhere, otherwise it would not be nonsense.

To summarize or to sum up the sense: everyone has to find out for themselves whether it makes sense to read these stories or to bring Uhlenspiegel together with a village of Schilda citizens. That in turn would then make sense. In this way, every reader would make sense of these stories (pardon interpret sense into them) where there was no sense before and it would have made sense (for everyone) to write or read these stories.

However, they should approach the sense and nonsense of these stories unencumbered (meaning already encumbered with sense but equipped with unencumbered senses).

With this in mind: lots of sense enjoyment.

*PS.1: Topical note

Perhaps this explains the phenomenon of dictatorships that is emerging again today. A single person (but with almost absolutely immovable sense) is confronted with a huge mass of people whose senses are rather dulled. A constellation that not only makes no sense, but makes (pardon contains) an incredibly dangerous sense. More than nonsense, much more, the strongest nonsense there can ever be.

PS.2: Reading recommendation

It may make sense to read only one story a month, or it may not make sense to read more than one story a month. That's why this book contains twelve stories. If you feel like reading more, you can of course read all twelve stories in one day instead of just one story a month.

You will want to get to the stories at last. Here you go. Have fun.

1.
Forward-looking penitence

*I*t so happened that Uhlenspiegel didn't know what to do with himself and the world on a Sunday and decided without further ado to do the same thing that very few people did on such a day. He thought he would meet his own kind, where there were few, these few had to be like him somehow, because there were not many of his kind on the globe.

He stepped out of the house indifferently and saw a not inconsiderable number of Schilda citizens hurrying towards the nearest inn. Towards them, like red-hot salmon, a few were making their way in the opposite direction. Uhlenspiegel followed them, although the pleasant smell of alcohol and the sound of the first chicken frying almost caught up with him. And who knows what Uhlenspiegel would have decided if these scents had reached his nose in time. As it was, he suddenly found himself standing in front of the church in Schilda, its entrance wide open like the mouth of the whale that had eaten Jonas.

From inside, the first sounds of the organ floated outside, mingling with incense and the occasional familiar sound of one coin falling on another.

Where money is concerned, it's good to follow the sound, thought Uhlenspiegel and stepped inside the huge old walls. A few souls remained huddled together on worm-eaten wooden benches and the priest stood in front in dark purple splendor with his neck proudly stretched, straight as a measuring stick.

When the singing began, Uhlenspiegel thought he could hear even fewer people than there actually were. The heavy organ sounds weighed like lead on the despondent voices of the penitent. Then the priest began. He made continuous signs in the air with his hands so that Uhlenspiegel thought he was painting pictures and had forgotten his brush and easel in his haste. His voice was well-rounded from years of excessive incense and his eyes, although they could hardly really see anything, looked like the eyes of an eagle that had spotted a victim.

From time to time, Uhlenspiegel heard words that he did not understand, a language that was old-fashioned to him. Then he heard the priest's speech all the more clearly again, and those present huddled together even more under his words as if they had to take cover so as not to be hit on the head by his skillful articulations. At the climax of the speech, the priest broke off and ran through the rows of pews with a tin in which coins were bouncing up and down.

Uhlenspiegel found himself in a quandary: he had no money in his pockets, nor had he seen a sign at the front door stating that admission was charged. In no time at all, the priest was standing in front of Uhlenspiegel with the full force of his body.

Everything here looks like a whale, thought Uhlenspiegel, the church with the cracked open door and now the priest, his face glowing red, standing in front of him with his mouth wide open.

Uhlenspiegel stretched out his hand and dropped something soft into the slot. The priest's eyes began to sparkle, missing the familiar jingling of the coins. Uhlenspiegel leaned over to the priest and whispered something in his ear. Soon the priest's face brightened. He unscrewed the lid of the tin and told Uhlenspiegel to reach in and take out a few coins so that he could eat something later at the inn, as he had thrown all his money, a colorful paper bill with endless numbers from a distant Arab country, into the box.

Uhlenspiegel took a liking to the whole affair; in his unrestrained imagination he could think of no other profession that suited his tastes better. One could walk around in elegant clothes, wallow in incense, paint all sorts of pictures in the air and, on top of that, give the audience a good talking to and, what struck Uhlenspiegel most strangely and pleasantly, they paid you money for being able to recite their list of sins to you. In the course of his life, Uhlenspiegel had long since discovered that where there was a top, there was also a top above it, and above this top there was another top, just like a ladder with endless rungs that eventually disappeared into the clouds of the sky.

He got himself some clothes that shone more than the priest's robes, adorned himself here and there with gold amulets, put his head under a venerable black hat and decided to pay the priest a visit.

Early one sunny morning, he rang the doorbell of the priest's house. The clergyman was extremely surprised by the visit, no news had reached him, otherwise there would certainly have been a princely meal with exquisite delicacies on the table.

Heaven bless you for your good intentions, Uhlenspiegel said unctuously. And so that it doesn't stop at good intentions, because you know that not only words but also deeds are weighed in gold in heaven, hurry to ask the housekeeper to coax the best dish from the kitchen, because this is how prophetic messengers have always been treated, as described everywhere in our thick book.

You could see that Uhlenspiegel had prepared himself well, at the word of the prophetic messenger the priest disappeared in a deeply bowed posture, it was a long time before he returned, the first fine odors were already clinging to his robe.

It troubles me, continued Uhlenspiegel, that you intend to deceive your superiors, he suddenly began.

The priest was frightened as hell, but one couldn't tell from his face whether there was a reason for it.

How is it that Your Highness assumes such a thing? he asked back boldly.

It is not up to me, replied Uhlenspiegel, to give you an answer. The deception will be found out. Tell me first whether you are the one in charge of the collection boxes.

The priest nodded somewhat hesitantly.

Fine, continued Uhlenspiegel, then you will be prepared to give all the money that is in the collection box so that I can bring it to the church myself.

Certainly, if Your Highness commands it.

That's where the deception lies! Uhlenspiegel shouted, there's a worthless piece of paper in the box that you think is a huge Arab banknote. Now the priest was really startled. There really was a prophetic messenger standing in front of him, how else could he know about the banknote? And he probably also knew that he wanted to take his own share of this small Arab treasure. Uhlenspiegel told him to open the box. In fact, the piece of paper turned out to be nothing but an Arab banknote with an infinite row of numbers.

I will give you the opportunity to ask pardon for your transgression, Uhlenspiegel told the trembling clergyman.

The trembling would not stop. All his life he had talked about prophets, clairvoyants and the like, but when he suddenly saw with his own eyes that someone could look into a sealed box and, what's more, read thoughts, he was terrified; he had never thought that such things could really happen.

Uhlenspiegel looked him sharply in the eye and snatched the piece of paper. He read out the long series of numbers meaningfully.

I will tell you the requirement for penance, said Uhlenspiegel. You are to pay the number I have read out to you to the church, but not with strange Arab coins, but with our familiar local gold coins.

The priest swallowed, which is why Uhlenspiegel felt compelled to dig more deeply.

All you have to do is preach your sermon more clearly, mention purgatory a little more, hold up a mirror to the transgressions of your flock and you will realize that the box is filling up faster than you can hear, the coins are jingling faster than your ears can distinguish their sound. And what you are unable to collect in this way, you should pay out of your piggy bank. You know best that everyone has to pay for their own mistakes.

This was decided by the foreign lord, who was no other than the spiritualized Uhlenspiegel. Of course, he would personally undertake to bring the sum to the church later. But the priest, in his guilt, did not even dare ask who this church was and where it was that Uhlenspiegel intended to take the money.

The trail left by the gold coins later pointed to a strange church of which Uhlenspiegel had spoken, in which juicy roasts sizzled on the spit, boot-high glasses of beer stood on the tables and attractively dressed female beings rushed through the waves of noisy conversation, satisfying the thirsty throats and growling stomachs, even the wide-open eyes.

One of these necks was tucked into a stiff, snow-white collar, from which a crimson robe fell down, covering the growling stomach that was probably most familiar to Uhlenspiegel himself.

2.
Robbed robbery

The citizens of Schilda lived in a happy state for a long, long time until one day they realized that they were working more and more every day without their possessions increasing to the same extent. Worse still, the more the good citizens of Schilda worked, the less and less money they had.

There must be a hole in our town, they thought. Where else would all the money go? But where was this hole? Doors and windows had been built in front of the openings of the houses so that nothing could escape. So, the hole had to be somewhere else. Either so small that you couldn't find it or so huge that you couldn't see anything because of the hole.

At this fateful hour, Uhlenspiegel came along the way. It was fortunate that he, too, was destitute because of a hole in his wallet. He could understand the citizens of Schilda only too well; their shared suffering brought them together, as did Uhlenspiegel's need to fill his purse again. This time, Uhlenspiegel had to work from the underground, as it were. He probably realized that not all the citizens of Schilda were destitute, certainly the majority, but the others could live in all the more luxury. He gathered all the poor creatures around him to share his wisdom with them.

Where have you taken all the money you have laboriously collected? Uhlenspiegel asked the group.

The answers were very diverse. The inn was mentioned, as well as a house with pretty women in it, the hairdresser and many more. And in between all this, the bench always appeared, not the four-legged wooden frame for sitting on, but the marble box (bank) where you went in with gold coins and came out with written pieces of paper. (Translator's note: the German word 'Bank' means both bench and bank.)

When Uhlenspiegel heard this, he scolded the citizens of Schilda. Had they never heard that from time to time robbers appeared out of nowhere, attracted by the magic of money, and loved to plunder such buildings? Even if it wasn't that he had heard of other robbers. The business of robbery was too tedious for them, and they had found that it was much easier to build a nice building and wait for the citizens to deliver on their own, so they didn't have to go to the trouble of robbing. And if the beautiful little bank in Schilda had never been the scene of the first event, it could only mean that they were dealing with the second kind.

Such talk was well received and Uhlenspiegel decided to go one better.

It is certainly unfair, he continued, to put all the blame on such robbery. He had found that the biggest hole was the biggest building and what was the biggest, apart from the church, which he did not want to talk about in this context, as it was a hole between earth and heaven where the treasures seeped so far away that they remained inaccessible from then on. Apparently, the priest had the treasures stored in an unknown building in heaven, although no-one knew how they disappeared into heaven for a short time.

Then the biggest building is the town hall, explained Uhlenspiegel, it's nothing more than a huge enclosed hole where all your money disappears.

Slowly it dawned on the citizens of Schilda, they thought of the many taxes and charges, charges here and charges there, not a day went by without this big hole spitting out a new charge, plus a few disgruntled faces to monitor and collect it all.

On my travels, I have found the happiest people were those who had no town hall in their town, continued Uhlenspiegel. Unfortunately, a long time ago, one city started this evil, which spread like a plague and soon infected the whole world except for a few small, blissful islands where there were no stones to erect such buildings with the money and sweat of the people living nearby.

Now that they had the town hall, they could not simply think it away. However, he recommended pooling all the money that was still available and sending all the councilors out into the wide world for three years to see how they could discover other forms and taxes that were not known in Schilda. In the meantime, Schilda would have become prosperous enough to be able to afford the councilors again, even if they had put even more crazy ideas into their heads in the meantime.

For the rest, they could consider during the three years whether it would not be better to live without the whole thing and the town hall could be converted into a cattle shed or something similar, with the oxen on the first floor, the donkeys on the second floor and the largest cattle at the top under the roof so as not to have too much conversion work.

It happened as they had discussed, and everything happened as Uhlenspiegel had foreseen in his wisdom. After a year, everyone possessed as much as they had never previously seen in their lives. Uhlenspiegel looked at the splendid prosperity for another year and then decided to get his fair share.

In the meantime, he had made himself comfortable in the town hall so that he could dine and spend the night in a different room every day and he called the citizens of Schilda together for an important announcement on the market square.

Every day I sit under the golden dome, Uhlenspiegel said, but not for my own pleasure. Rather, I observe everything that happens around Schilda. You mustn't think that the others haven't heard of your wealth. All sorts of riff-raff are on the move, not a few robbers among them, to rob you of what you have earned. The speech had the desired effect and the citizens of Schilda were thrown into complete confusion. They had just become accustomed to prosperity and were about to lose it again? Uhlenspiegel made every effort to restore calm.

You must hide the most valuable things where they are least expected. And where is such a place? Right where it is most visible, at the top of the tallest trees. Pack everything of value in green sacks so that they are not discovered immediately and climb the highest trees, tying the sacks to the treetops. I have already selected suitable trees and marked them clearly for you. But now we have to take precautions in case a robber deviates from his habit of looking down, because the treasures are usually buried in the ground, and discovers the sacks in the trees. He will not think that you have hidden rags in them and will immediately climb the tree. You must take precautions against this. By sawing a piece out of the tree, just big enough that you can't climb from one end to the other, twice as big as a common robber is usually tall. However, when the robbers hear you sawing, they will be attracted by the strange noises. Once you have cut out the piece, run into your houses immediately without looking back. Think of Lot's wife if you don't want to end up as a pillar of salt. Don't be alarmed if you hear a terrible noise immediately afterwards. It's the robbers breaking through the undergrowth in a hurry. Nothing will happen to you, you have locked yourselves in your houses. And your treasures are safe because no-one can climb a tree with a piece missing in the middle.

That's what happened. The most valuable pieces were hung in green sacks on the trees and at the same time a large piece was cut out of each tree. Then the Schilda citizens rushed off, faster than a tree could topple.

Uhlenspiegel only had to pick up what he could carry away. The damage was quickly forgotten, however, as the citizens of Schilda still had two bearable years ahead of them – thanks to the unexpectedly blessed one-year delay in the return of their councilors – in which they once again achieved unparalleled wealth without a town hall and councilors.

3.

A topsy-turvy world - for those who like it

When Uhlenspiegel was looking for a pastime, he remembered the citizens of Schilda and the many pleasant encounters, even if they were more pleasant as far as he was concerned. So he decided to pay the town another visit. He put on a distinguished tailcoat, so that one might have thought one was looking at an important scholar, artist, poet or the like, put his rucksack not on his back but under his coat, like a hump as a sign that despite all his elegance he was marked by the burden of life, grabbed a walking stick with a gold-speckled knob and set off.

On top of his head, he wore a top hat that measured at least a meter high. But the wind didn't like this and blew it off his head time and time again. Uhlenspiegel therefore became very disgruntled, especially at the wind, and arrived in Schilda in this mood. The first thing he saw there was an old mill, which, driven by the storm, rotated violently and caused even more turbulence in the air. Uhlenspiegel ran straight to the blacksmith, borrowed the strongest chain he could get and returned to the mill. He positioned himself in front of the mill and, like a lasso, tried to catch a windmill sail with the chain. After a short time, a large number of the citizens of Schilda had gathered to watch the strange goings-on. Uhlenspiegel pretended not to notice all this and intensified his efforts to catch a windmill sail with the iron chain.

When another gust of wind swept over his head and tore the magnificent top hat into the mud, he stamped on the ground like Rumpelstiltskin and insulted the windmill in the worst possible way.

After making a right impression behind his back in this way, he turned around and let his eyes circle in surprise, as if he thought he had been fighting the windmill alone the whole time. Suddenly, he mysteriously put his finger over his mouth and motioned the citizens of Schilda to come closer.

He must not speak loudly, he whispered, because he had discovered a great and even more wondrous secret. The world was upside down, to a certain extent, and many things were not what they appeared to be. The moon was nothing other than the sun which had put on a different garment, just as every sensible person dressed differently for the night than for their daytime activities. And the rare hours when the moon and sun can be seen at the same time are nothing more than optical illusions, mirages, just as he had encountered them on his distant journeys in the desert. The windmills, however, are nothing more than transformed monsters that could turn into a dragon or something similar at any time. They only rotated in order to make people dependent through feigned work and then, when it suited them, to fail to work and bring hardship and hunger upon venerable citizens.

He had also discovered that it was not the wind that turned the mills, but the other way round, the mills were constantly turning in circles to generate wind and thus maltreat respectable citizens like him by blowing the hats off their heads and, if they were not careful and did not cover their ears at the right moment, blowing their minds away by going in one ear and out the other. Over time, many things have been turned upside down because nobody appreciates the good old things anymore. And these distortions had become so brazen that the whole world would have to be shaken up to restore order.

At this moment, a dog barked, which upset Uhlenspiegel, as someone had the audacity to disturb his important speech by barking, but at the same time it suited him. He had the dog brought to him and grabbed it by the ears and tail, lamenting how the world had been turned upside down because people were afraid of being bitten by a four-legged friend when fear should be different. He also wanted to start right away to set everything right again, for which, in order to make a start, this dog had to be bitten hard so that it would understand the right order, gain respect for people and, as a result of the salutary instruction, spread it among its fellow dogs.

For him, this task was beneath his station, as he had gained respect from a lion only a year ago on his last journey by showing him his teeth and biting his ear. The poor fellow had then fled in horror and only dared to stop again when he had long since left the jungle and found himself in another desert, namely the ice desert. Uhlenspiegel was told about the strange appearance of a lion in the Arctic Ocean, which did not surprise him, as the lion had fled so far from him.

When the reason for this strange event was discovered, he was given the honor of naming this lion, which now lives in the eternal ice, and he decided on sea lion, as there is more water up there than desert sand. Now, however, there was no longer any hesitation in teaching this dog the proper respect for the human creature and someone brave should step forward to bite the dog hard on its backside before it dared to do such a thing to a human being.

As no-one was to be found, Uhlenspiegel turned to the mayor, who had also arrived in the meantime, but as an honorable politician, he was to be the champion of this good cause. What was the poor man to do, whether he wanted to or not, he found himself caught up in Uhlenspiegel's speech, stepped forward amidst the din from the others and bit the kicking dog's backside to Uhlenspiegel's delight. Not without the dog emitting something dark from very close to the bite, which spread a foul odor to at least drive away the mayor's biting head.

Uhlenspiegel gave the animal another mighty kick, unfortunately at the site of the bite, which in turn enraged the dog so much that it attacked the mayor's leg. Obviously, the mayor had not bitten hard enough and therefore had not earned enough respect.

Now there was great excitement, a wild chaos broke out, everyone rushed at the dog and thus also at the mayor, who soon found himself under a huge mountain of people throwing punches. In the end, both the dog and the mayor were badly maltreated, but this earned Uhlenspiegel's appreciation for having fought for the good cause.

However, the incident showed how right he was and that this four-legged friend had been taught excessive respect in several ways. Therefore, everyone should swarm out and proceed as the mayor had heroically shown them. But he would come back the next day to explain other important, twisted things to them.

And so it happened, both the swarming out of the citizens of Schilda and the return of Uhlenspiegel, who appeared punctually on the market square the next morning and looked into quite a few scratched faces.

Despite the events, almost all the citizens of Schilda had turned up. It sounded too important, what Uhlenspiegel wanted to tell. He also exuded a strange aura called attraction, which could neither be seen nor felt, but was simply there.

Uhlenspiegel wore his huge top hat, stood upright on the market platform, surveyed the crowd with his eyes and suddenly struck a blow with his arm as if he wanted to divide the air. And he wanted to divide, not the air, there was enough of that, it didn't need to be divided, he divided the citizens of Schilda into a right and a left side.

After creating a respectable alleyway between the two halves with just a wave of his hand, he explained to the right side that they had failed to continue the fight against the windmills because of the urgent problem with the dogs. They might turn back into monsters at any time or generate such a strong wind that the whole of Schilda would be swept off the face of the earth.

However, he was only afraid that the expensive top hat would be blown off his head once again, perhaps the turning of the windmill was the last straw that caused the wind barrel to overflow and his hat to fall off his head. He therefore ordered one half to equip themselves with chains and bind the windmill from top to bottom in order to be armed against monsters, storms and the like. In the meantime, he wanted to tell the others other important things, from which everyone would benefit, and the others would, as it were, prepare a reward for the brave windmill fighters.

Something happened to me, Uhlenspiegel began his new speech, just as I set foot in your village. I saw a magnificent apple tree, the likes of which I had never seen before. Such color. Round fruits, golden yellow, glistening in the sun, inviting the weary wanderer to feast on them, to draw new strength. And me? In my good nature, I responded and sampled an apple. But instead of thinking of honey, sweet rolls and the like, a sour lemon came to my mind as I bit into the apple. Uhlenspiegel said this in a drawn-out, weighty tone, giving the citizens of Schilda time to get a really bad conscience, as the apple tree belonged to them. And wasn't it pathetic and disgraceful to receive an honorable, tired wanderer in this way?

What can the poor tree do about it, continued Uhlenspiegel. You don't get sweet just from the sun, or has anyone ever licked a ray of sunshine and realized that it tastes like sugar?

You just have to water it properly, said Uhlenspiegel. Instead of making all sorts of pointless things like sweets, which are just an example of things that are upside down; you think you're eating the sweets, but instead they eat you up, starting with your teeth, where they eat big holes in them. What can I tell you, instead of making this sweet corruption to enjoy its vice, you should water your apple trees with sugar water until it comes out of their ears. Then you will have the sweetest apples, and on top of that you will get your sugar back when you munch the apples, and besides that, why do you eat sweet and sour one after the other, first the sour apple and then the sweet candy, when you can eat both together in a much more practical way?

The citizens of Schilda didn't really understand his words, but that didn't matter, as the most important of them, the nature citizens, had decided to eat only plant-based foods, as Uhlenspiegel's words suited them very well.

And so Uhlenspiegel didn't even have to continue, because one of the nature citizens immediately suggested collecting all the sweets and giving them to Uhlenspiegel, who was to use them to make water for all the trees.

It went very well, and the juggler only wanted to insist on a small modification as, strangely enough, he liked everything sweet except brown chocolate. Uhlenspiegel praised the citizens of Schilda for their suggestion and zeal and said that they should consider that it was a great inconvenience to have to pour chocolate and cocoa into the milk at breakfast in the morning. All you had to do was forbid the cows to continue eating grass and stuff them full of chocolate, then it would only be a matter of time before they delivered finished cocoa and not milk, and if you rushed the cows through the village before milking them until they rolled their eyes from the heat, they would also deliver warm chocolate, as it should be for breakfast, without having to laboriously heat it on the stove.

In general, said Uhlenspiegel, there was a lot wrong with the cows and a lot needed to be changed. It makes no sense for them all to moo in the same key. Rather, the cattle should be taught that each one uses a different tone for its mooing. This would make it easier for everyone, especially the blind, to tell them apart. It would also soon sound so interesting in Schilda that they could save themselves the trouble of torturing their children to learn to play musical instruments in order to organize concerts later on, for which everyone would have to pay dearly, as the bellowing of the cows would be sweeter and more varied than a choir of angels in their ears.

With this heavenly prospect and a bulging sack full of delicious sweets, Uhlenspiegel climbed down from the market platform. The citizens of Schilda had enough work to do for the time being, while he would have to set off to discover new and interesting things for them in the world, of course only after the effort of making sugary water to pour on the apple trees.

4.

Christmas – beneath the earth's surface

With the cleverness of their minds and the diligence of their hands, the citizens of Schilda had ensured that the largest sign erected by human hands was located in their town. High enough to be seen even from the opposite side of the globe. At least that was the opinion of their cleverest man, whom they had appointed mayor of their small town due to his immense intellect.

Come Christmas time, however, even the smallest Christmas tree on earth was easier to see than the sign, because now every tree had brightly lit candles, while the immeasurably high sign was nothing more than a long, black line that was lost in the darkness of the night. Now advice was at a premium. After all, anyone who had become accustomed to being the best and highest of all places over the long year, even if it was only because of a sign, could not possibly benefit from losing this honor at Christmas of all times.

In every little house, heads were smoldering, most of all the one on the mayor's shoulders. It soon paid off that they had elected their smartest man as their leader. He had summoned the citizens to the market square for an important announcement on the morrow.

The following day, people stood expectantly and densely packed in the center of their small town.

We will have to remedy this evil, said the mayor in a way that is as simple as it is logical, this is the result of my long nights of thinking how to solve the unspeakable problem.

The tension rose to an unbearable level with these words, so that the mayor felt compelled to come up with the solution without further ado if he didn't want to risk a terrible storm over his city, such was the crackling tension in the air.

If we have the highest sign, then we also need the biggest Christmas tree in order not to lose our position among all the cities.

A huge murmur went through the audience. The cleverness of the solution had almost overwhelmed everyone, causing mouths to open wide and astonished eyes to stare throughout the day.

As circumstances would have it, the tallest Christmas tree was also in their town. It was a magnificent tree, thick green needles with huge cones, which had not accepted being topped by a ridiculous sign and had therefore grown almost to the clouds in recent years.

Now the solution had been found, but not yet the way to implement the mayor's wise advice.

We will, the mayor continued, only light the top with candles. We can't possibly put candles on the whole tree. Even if we started at the beginning of the year, we wouldn't be finished by Christmas. Nor does our hard-pressed city budget, which has had huge holes eaten into it by the cost of the tall sign, allow for such a solution. It is enough to decorate the top, just the size of a standard Christmas tree. The whole thing still remained the tallest festive tree on the face of the earth.

However, these additional words had neither found the solution nor made the work any easier. No-one dared to climb the tall tree. An evil Christmas spirit could be hiding at the top. It was also possible to get lost in the tall tree and not find your way back to earth. Or someone could even accidentally end up on the other side of the earth while climbing up and never see their beloved home again in their life.

One of the citizens suggested that the tree should be shown respect. Everyone should bow to the mayor in an appropriate manner, why shouldn't the Christmas tree too?

At first, nobody really knew what to make of these words until the speaker felt compelled to explain further.

If the tree bowed in reverence to its mayor, it would just be an opportunity to seize it by its crown and add candles to the top of the Christmas tree.

Everyone understood, and everyone was so impressed that it was decided to make the speaker the new mayor, should the old one suffer or die in this dangerous undertaking. For might it not be that the tree bowed so low that it broke apart and crushed their beloved mayor? The idea was refined in many ways. First, a throne was built, and a crown was placed on the mayor's head, because shouldn't the bow of a king be lower than that of a mayor? The tree would not notice the deception. In addition, ten strong men were chosen and provided with strong ropes to tie the tree down once it had bowed to the ground. In this way, they could decorate it in peace and quiet and let it rise again slowly enough, otherwise it could end up extinguishing the painstakingly placed candles when it quickly shot up.

Everything was ready. The mayor sat on a magnificent throne with a crown on his head in front of the huge Christmas tree, with ten strong men at his side. Now it had to be explained to the tree that it had to bow with obeisance before the Supreme Lord of Schilda, the temporary Christmas king born of necessity, so to speak.

A speech was prepared for this, which it was the task of the town treasurer to deliver. It is not appropriate to reproduce it here, as it contained countless examples of the extraordinary nature of the small town, the incomparable achievements of its brave mayor and concluded with the words:

May we now ask you, like everyone else, to bow before the Christmas King, who in a sense is also the supreme employer of all Christmas trees and therefore also your supreme employer and pay your respects to him.

Once again, there was tremendous tension in the air, everyone was looking at the tree. For minutes, hours, days. But nothing happened. Undaunted, the mayor held on to his throne until it finally dawned on him that there was no glory to be won this way.

An excited discussion broke out about the reasons for the failure of their endeavor. The city treasurer might have spoken too softly. Nobody knew how far up the Christmas tree its ears were attached. Perhaps the city treasurer had just spoken in the wrong language, which the tree could not understand despite his Christmas efforts. There was no way around thinking about another solution.

If the tree doesn't come to us, one of us will come to it, shouted an agitated citizen.

Nobody understood. Climbing up the tree had already been rejected as too dangerous.

So this speaker also felt compelled to carry out his idea. If the tree grew as high as the sky, one of them could do the same. And once he was as tall as the tree, it would be easy to attach the lights to the top.

This suggestion met with no less enthusiasm than the first. They quickly found one of their own, who was already taller than the others. He was placed on a chair to make him comfortable, but in the open air, for how else could he grow in a house where he would soon hit his head against the ceiling.

A path was laid out from each store to this chair, so that all kinds of delicacies could be brought in sufficient quantity and conveniently. After all, the chosen one would have to eat well in order to grow tall. A lively discussion also broke out as to which culinary delights were most suitable for the purpose.

One swore by yellow turnips, because every time he ate one of them, despite their unpleasant taste, he woke up the next morning the same length taller as the yellow turnip had been.

Many other wondrous recipes were divulged, often encouraging the consumption of pine cones, because after all, the aim was to catch up with the tree along its length, to take it by the horns, and in the case of a tree, these were represented by its cones, as nothing else comparable to horns could be found on a Christmas tree. In their thoroughness, the citizens of this strange place thought of everything, even of digging a narrow ditch from the chair to a sufficiently distant field. Because where a lot of food was eaten, a lot had to be disposed of.

Soon after, the undertaking began. Food was brought in by the bucketful and, when the natural course could not manage it on its own, it was stuffed into the chosen one with funnels and rammers, so that one might have thought one was watching the fattening of a Christmas goose. After every hour, the chosen one had to stand up, firstly to allow the food to sink down more easily, and secondly to measure the extent to which the first success had already been achieved. However, there was no sign of this. Not after an hour, not after a day, not even after a week or a month.

Some people were already saying that the result resembled a balloon about to burst. Others, on the other hand, also saw this from the practical side. Then the chosen one would just have to be laid down, he would grow more in width than in height, so the width would grow in height.

When, after another month, on the morning of a lovely summer's day, the chosen one no longer stirred and his mouth could no longer be opened, even with the greatest force, and finally, as an unmistakable sign of his death, there was nothing more to be disposed of through the channel behind the chair, the undertaking was ended. He was given a stately funeral, as he had sacrificed himself for the glory of the town and had not put his own well-being above anything else.

It took three days to dig a sufficiently large pit, and the pit had to be somewhat larger if the deceased decided to turn over in his grave, which was mentioned on many occasions. The bakers, butchers and farmers mourned the deceased, and the capital invested in vain in a special way, and they were given the honor of sitting in the front row during the mourners' gathering to see the result of their efforts for as long as possible.

After an appropriate period of mourning, it just so happened that the mayor had the idea for the best of all solutions during that dark time of mourning. He explained that it had come to him while digging during those three days. All you had to do was dig a pit directly under the tree, deep enough for the tree to reach the top. This way, its candles could be conveniently lit, and it would only have to be lifted up again afterwards. Once again, it turned out that they had chosen their cleverest as mayor. The spades were still warm from digging and they immediately began to carry out the plan.

In the end, no-one could remember how long they had been digging. But they could remember the tremendous noise when the earth gave way and the huge tree disappeared into the hole. And much deeper than expected. The citizens of that wondrous place realized that it was impossible to ever bring it back to the surface. So, one of their own was lowered down into the hole on a long rope, at least to decorate the top of the tree with candles. Even if they didn't have the tallest Christmas tree, they would have the lowest. And no-one had ever heard of one that lit up underground. Even the strange but well-traveled journeyman Uhlenspiegel, who visited their tranquil little town from time to time, had never heard of such a Christmas tree deep in the ground during his many visits.

Incidentally, the highest sign on this globe could still be referred to. If the opportunity arose, a note would be placed at the top of the sign stating that this is also the lowest Christmas tree in the world. Anyone who doesn't believe it should set off in good time, the note on the sign can be seen far enough away, and no assurances can yet be given as to how long the candles on the lowest Christmas tree in the world will burn. For this reason, it was necessary to hurry to be able to admire it at Christmas time.

5.

The new (topsy-turvy) world

*U*hlenspiegel was annoyed at always having to walk to Schilda to have fun. He noticed that his bones weren't getting any younger and the journeys weren't getting any shorter or less arduous. With the signs of age, the pleasure of traveling became a displeasure, and he thought about making it more comfortable in this respect too.

Although the citizens of Schilda could be persuaded to do all sorts of strange things in their town, Uhlenspiegel did not know how he would succeed in luring them away from the tranquility of their small town. The calculation was simple. If he could no longer go to Schilda, the others had to come to him or spread out into the world in such a way that they could be found in every place, including the places where Uhlenspiegel lived and the villages immediately around him.

Now it was no easy task to lure the citizens of Schilda out of their tranquil world. A number of thoughts came to Uhlenspiegel's mind. He rejected them all, none of them seemed suitable for his plan. He thought of sending them out into the world as master builders, introducing the building of town halls without doors and windows everywhere. But he rejected this idea too. Not because there would be no light in the town halls. Rather, how were all the high gentlemen supposed to get into the town hall to govern the ordinary people if the town halls were built without doors and windows.

He discarded several more such suggestions until he simply set off, trusting that the right thing would creep into his mind along the way. On the way, Uhlenspiegel's heart did somersaults, life seemed so beautiful to him, the sun was shining, the birds were chirping, flowers exuded their scent, and the beautifully cleaned villages gleamed in the bright daylight. His soul wanted to overflow, and he was almost about to renounce all his mischief and start a better life. Only it occurred to him that the weather would change, rain instead of sun, gray walls instead of shining villages, so it would take something like merry pranks to bring a little light into the world.

As he turned somersaults, more inwardly than outwardly, Uhlenspiegel couldn't help but look at the world from below and realized how much more interesting it suddenly looked. The trees resembled frayed spoons, houses were like a sharp wedge with which someone was drilling holes in the air, clouds were an airy carpet, birds were black monsters racing along the ground, flowers resembled fine wine glasses.

You have to turn everything upside down, thought Uhlenspiegel, until you get tired of it. With these thoughts, he reached Schilda. He immediately made arrangements to see the mayor, as he had an important plan to present. Luckily for him, for not so long there had been another mayor, who no longer remembered the nasty pranks. The new mayor also seemed open to all things new, seeing this as an opportunity to dispel the old stink a little. Uhlenspiegel ran into open doors, met with wide-open ears and by the end of the conversation was no less than the mayor's first deputy. At a late hour and in rare harmony, the two went to the Ratskeller (a restaurant in the basement of the town hall) to discuss the new era over a nice glass of beer.

Everything must change, Uhlenspiegel began, everything, not a single thing must remain as it is. I have traveled the world a lot and have seen the new era everywhere. It wears splendid clothes, the new era, golden, trimmed with fine lace, overloaded with sparkling gemstones, you just have to get it right. On the other hand, it could even happen that the new era rolls over you and leaves nothing behind from Schilda but a heap of flattened houses. You have to come at the right time, this is the new motto, otherwise you will be punished by life, which is kind to the brave but cruel to latecomers. Reason and order were needed everywhere, such strange things as town halls without windows, without doors and the like should no longer be allowed to exist.

Discussed, decided, done. The new mayor and Uhlenspiegel transformed Schilda from top to bottom, and vice versa, from bottom to top, so that it soon became unrecognizable and was nothing more than a small town like millions of others. Everything was normal as in the world, but for the citizens of Schilda, normal was like a completely new world. And Uhlenspiegel had had nothing else in mind.

Time had become normal, but it was nowhere near as golden, lace-covered and gemstone-laden as advertised. Soon nobody felt comfortable in Schilda anymore, but there was nothing left to change. Uhlenspiegel therefore called a large meeting to announce to everyone what solution he had found to the new problems.

Dear citizens of Schilda, Uhlenspiegel began his pompous speech, dear citizens and non-citizens of Schilda, we cannot undo what we have had to change and what has caused us so much trouble. Even if the times do not yet seem as golden, lace-studded and jeweled as expected, we are on the right path, but it will not be any different in its way than when we started to change it. That's why I recommend everyone to let Schilda be Schilda and go out into the wide world. I myself have been there several times, in the wide world, and have gained a lot each time, gained experience, impressions, money and (Uhlenspiegel only mumbled this to himself) also fun.

That's why I advise each and every one of you to go out into the world and take your experience as a citizen of Schilda with you. You will not only be welcomed with open arms but placed where you deserve to be. In leading positions, especially the important ones in town halls and the like. Since you are, so to speak, the only ones who know how to bring light into these dark buildings. Everywhere you will plant the seeds for a new Schilda and, if you like, you can consider coming together again after your work is done. Now it must end, it is hard for me to think of leaving you. But we will meet again, in the real world, as truly as I stand here.

Uhlenspiegel ended there. He had had nothing else in mind but to watch the goings-on of Schilda grow all over the world. So in his old age, he no longer had to bother traveling to Schilda, but could find it everywhere, even in his closest surroundings, called home, to have fun until his own end.

Everything else happened as Uhlenspiegel had predicted. The citizens of Schilda left their place to see the wide world, were welcomed with open arms, and even more, especially in town halls and similar places, were placed in the most important positions, enriching life everywhere with their blunt minds.

6.
Fairytale freedom

The citizens of Schilda lived so much in their own world that not even fairy tales had reached them. Not far from their tranquility, Uhlenspiegel got out of bed one morning, and as it was on the wrong side, he was overcome by a rather grim feeling. His first glance fell on an old book of fairy tales, courtesy of the Grimm brothers.

Grimm, murmured Uhlenspiegel, it comes more rightly to me at this unhappy moment than anything else in the world. Isn't it enough to have to get up in the morning just because someone thought of inventing work for the world?

And in such a hurry that his own feet are overturned and his left foot kicks the sleeping mother earth first. Such thoughts made his face a good deal grimmer as he leafed through the worn book.

The next day, Uhlenspiegel set off for Schilda, carrying a huge bag of utensils on his back, but hardly any of them in the way one usually carries them when traveling.

As soon as he arrived in Schilda, he stopped in front of the first house, reached into the bulging cloth sack and pulled out a hammer, nails and an old dry sugar packet.

The citizen of Schilda residing there was astonished when he heard the strange woodpecker's tapping, and even more so when he saw Uhlenspiegel going about his strange business. Behind him, his wife rushed outside and when Uhlenspiegel saw her, long, pointed fingernails, a razor-sharp chin and disheveled hair, he saw himself confirmed in doing his work here. The man's dismay immediately subsided after Uhlenspiegel explained the reason for his work. He pointed to the old book, then to the picture of two wandering children breaking gingerbread from a house.

It could well happen, Uhlenspiegel remarked, that one of your children gets lost. In such cases, it would be more than appropriate to have a house covered in confectionery. Everyone knows how good a person's nose is and how surely children would be attracted to such sweet treats, the sweet smell of which they are still able to perceive from the other side of the world.

Of course, to give the whole thing a real effect, the sugar would have to be broken out in places. In the end, the starving children would not dare to take a bite if the whole thing was intact in its perfect form. But once a start had been made, which, by the way, he would offer to do, it would take away all the children's fears. Also, the sweet scent would flow especially from the broken parts and would make it much easier for the children to find their way.

It doesn't take much imagination to picture what other stories Uhlenspiegel drew from the book to make good use of it. Soon Schilda resembled a colorful stew in which someone had mixed together all the vegetables he could get hold of. Women let their long blond hair hang out of the window, girls walked around in red bonnets, old wrinkled women constantly pestered and kissed toads, the mayor's wife stood on the balcony of the town hall, shaking feather beds from evening to morning to conjure up cooling snow in summer, haggard old men danced around a fire like Indian warriors, sang strange melodies and stamped their legs so hard that you would have thought the earth was shattering. Pigs stuck to geese and these in turn stuck to cows, and those who were lucky enough to escape all this absurdity were carried to their final resting place in large glass structures with a red apple stuck in their throats for all to see.

Uhlenspiegel watched the goings-on and took advantage here and there. Later, evil tongues claimed that he once even snatched the apple from the mouth of a dead man to satisfy his sudden hunger for fruit.

Uhlenspiegel slowly grew tired of it all and so he asked the citizens of Schilda to gather on the market square the next evening, by which time darkness must have fallen over Schilda. And so it happened. There was complete darkness, with only the moon peeking out from time to time, curious to see what Uhlenspiegel was going to do next.

He was already in the middle of a weighty speech that was increasingly turning into a fairytale-like story. While reading the book, he had noticed that some pages had been torn out and his suspicions had immediately led him to believe that it must be a particularly gruesome story with an even more miraculous ending. Diligent research on his part had confirmed this and, after much effort, he had come into possession of those pages, which had been found in ten pillows of an underly-overly-cautious journeyman teacher. However, the citizens of Schilda had now been sufficiently tested and deemed worthy enough to listen to the story by a self-proclaimed specialist in grim fairy tales.

To put it in a nutshell, dear citizens of Schilda, whispered Uhlenspiegel into the black night, this story was about a dragon that had seven heads and three times as many tongues on a single neck. The whole thing is not worth mentioning further, because such a dragon usually can't decide which head should get its turn to eat first, so it was usually only a matter of time before it starved to death.

If only there wasn't the little matter of spitting fire, a bad habit that he, Uhlenspiegel, could not approve of at all. Now this dragon, when it wasn't trying to eat a random passer-by, had the bad habit of spitting its fire everywhere, like someone who did the same with his saliva because he had too much of it in his own mouth.

At this point, Uhlenspiegel took a break. He told those present to be patient for a few moments, they would soon find out why.

Uhlenspiegel had not been gone five minutes when the first glimmers of light flickered from the town hall. Soon, the crackling could be heard getting louder and meter-high flames shot up from previously non-existent openings.

You don't have to think that fairy tales are a figment of the imagination, shouted Uhlenspiegel into the din of the flames. They are more real than you can imagine, as anyone can easily see.

He had just seen the seven-headed dragon breathing fire into the town hall, just as if one of them had been annoyed by one of the councilors' decisions.

But look at the happy ending! cried Uhlenspiegel, as befits any fairy tale. For all the nonsensical decrees, superfluous laws, puffed-up lists of sins, all the unnecessary forms that have maltreated you for a lifetime have been consumed by the flames and tomorrow, tomorrow, a free life will begin for you.

Those were his last words, at least for a considerable time to come, for Uhlenspiegel preferred to get out of the flaming dust, to preserve his own freedom, which as such, through his incomparable kindness, would also find its way into Schilda the next day.

7.
Horse mobile

*I*t was exactly seven years ago to the day that a rather angular box on four wheels rolled through Schilda without being tied to a horse or oxen. It took the first six years to recover from the wondrous scare, but then people began to think all the harder about how something similar could be achieved, as it would save cows and horses and eliminate the need to collect the large brown horse droppings.

One of them, and he was therefore one of the most respected inhabitants of the town, had come a long way in his life, to the town beyond the next one to be precise. An outstanding achievement, as only a few were allowed to leave the confines of their peaceful town. And it was also dangerous, only three of the few had found their way back to Schilda, the others had been swallowed up by the big, dangerous world.

The returnee had not seen a comparable vehicle on his journey, but he had seen a book with an illustration that resembled such a vehicle. And he knew about the words written underneath the picture with the significant information that such a vehicle had 20 horsepower. This excited the astonished minds. A rolling vehicle with 20 horses harnessed in front of it was something they had never heard of before. Harnessed in front of it. This is where the first, virtually insurmountable problem arose.

How could such a vehicle move with the power of 20 horses when there was simply no horse to be seen? Not to be seen, but all the more to be heard, which in turn meant that the 20 horses must be hidden in the vehicle. And that in turn could only be explained by special, particularly small horses, because 20 of them had to fit into the front box of the vehicle. The citizens of Schilda decided to follow in the footsteps of the rest of the world and build such a carriage on 80 horse legs.

Now it took 20 special horses to carry out such an undertaking. The citizens of Schilda benefited from their powers of observation, as they had long noticed that the cleverest of them also had the cleverest children. And those who were not born clever and acquired cleverness through all kinds of reading could also expect to call their offspring clever creatures. Which meant nothing more than selecting 20 horses that possessed all the necessary prerequisites or at least training them with the rest so that the next generation of horses could draw on the full potential. The most important thing was the size, the small size, 20 of them had to fit into the small box. To this end, 20 stables were built, new ones every day, a little smaller each day, to lock up the selected animals. The last stall would be no bigger than a shoebox; they would manage to trim the oversized creatures down to the required size.

During the time when they were not locked up, they had to learn to move in perfect unison and make sounds similar to the rolling vehicle, as far as one could still remember the noises. Similarly, none of them were allowed to excrete horse droppings. The well-traveled citizen agreed with the other representatives of the town that he could not remember this rolling vehicle dropping brown lumps behind it. Sure, it might stink in another way, but not from horse droppings.

The town's doctor was asked how this could be achieved, and he recommended a special diet that completely dissolved inside the animals except for the steam that escaped from the front and back. A steam diet plan was then drawn up with peas, beans and other legumes, which had to be meticulously adhered to. To be on the safe side, a fine net was placed around the rear of the animals, which only allowed steam to escape, not coarse particles, let alone large brown lumps. It is not reported whether a rolling, stinking vehicle on four wheels ever passed through this strange place again. Nor were the citizens of Schilda ever spared the hissing of a black monster on rails or the flying glass bird in the air to rack their brains as to how such creations could be recreated.

Soon their thoughts turned to the rolling square vehicle, but time had been turned back considerably. There were probably no longer any horses big enough to sit on or harness to a carriage and loaded hay wagons. And so the citizens of Schilda considered it a personal honor to harness themselves to such vehicles from time to time and stomp through their no longer so tranquil town to the sound of wild hoofbeats and neighing roars.

8.
Catching the wind at Schilda

*I*n Schilda, the time had long since passed when all work was carried out using only muscle power. The town's mills were driven by the power of the wind, one even by a stream that had been diverted for this purpose. It is no longer possible to say from where this invention was brought to Schilda, perhaps even by the wind itself, as there was no place on the globe where it did not blow. This was also the problem.

There was one place where the wind wasn't blowing, and it hadn't been seen for weeks in Schilda. A small troop of particularly courageous men was therefore put together to search the surrounding area for the missing wind. They were also equipped with various weapons in case they came across an unknown force that had captured the wind. They also carried a large linen cloth in case the wind was in a weakened state and had to be carried after being freed.

After a few days, the men returned, tired and weary, but without the wind. They had experienced every conceivable hardship and had to fight against forces that were raging out there in the world and of which nobody in Schilda had any idea. They had fought successfully, as their living return testified, but unfortunately without the wind.

In the meantime, a great deal of dust had been stirred up over the vanished wind, more than the wind itself had ever managed. Now, to make matters worse, the flour was slowly running out, also because the mills were no longer turning and the stream, having not been needed in the watermill for years, had changed its course out of annoyance at its dismissal and flooded the small village from time to time, much to everyone's irritation. But unlike its distant relative, the Nile, which brought rich fertilizer for the fields when it flooded, the small stream discharged foul-smelling mud, which remained hidden in the furthest cracks of the cellar for years and stank with relish, waiting for a visit from the next flood.

Action had to be taken. As quickly as possible. They suspected that the wind was secretly sneaking through the village at night and therefore decided to build a trap to confront it about this strange behavior. To this end, ropes, nets and cords were stretched between all the chimneys and roof ridges, in which the nocturnal prowler would get caught. However, so that success could be ascertained immediately, the ends of the ropes were tied around the bells that went round the necks of the cows. The four-legged animals were forbidden to move at night under penalty of punishment, so that the ringing of the cowbells would be an unmistakable sign when the wind had been caught.

It remained quiet for a long time until suddenly a violent commotion broke out. However, as none of the cowbells rang, there was no need to investigate the cause. The citizens of Schilda were all the more astonished when they saw the next morning that all the cows were hanging motionless in the air, on roofs, chimneys, between the houses and staring at the bells on their necks with wide, lifeless eyes.

The wind had played a terrible trick on them. Now they not only lacked flour, but also milk. Nevertheless, they decided to bravely continue the fight.

But first, out of sheer desperation, they tried to drive the mills with their own power; the hunger was too severe, grain had to be ground again at last. Every citizen of Schilda, big and small, stood in a curved line in front of the town's mills and blew with all their might. The few cows that had not witnessed the unspeakable night outside and had slept through the disaster in the barn were placed upside down in the row to support the effort from time to time.

It was no use, the sails wouldn't budge an inch and the people of Schilda were awestruck by the power of the wind. It could only be overcome with cunning and trickery, the power was on its side.

Once again, the city benefited from having elected its smartest person as mayor.

The wind is there, and it is not there, he began his speech. Anyway, it's there at night without us noticing. It flies past our mills without turning them. Instead, it hangs our cows on ropes and lets them dangle from the roofs. We will build a big wall around Schilda. A gate at one end to get in, a gate at the other end to get out. Now all we have to do is have two strong men hide on the exit gate at night and, if the wind tries to sneak away again, simply catch it by throwing down a large cloth.

A few minor problems and questions still needed to be clarified: Why didn't they catch the wind right at the entrance gate?

The mayor's answer was that it still had too much power. It should first let off steam in Schilda, so it would be easier to catch.

Was it the right wind? A night wind would only work at night, which meant that the millers and bakers would have to work at night in future.

This sacrifice could be endured if necessary.

And how did the wind know which was the entrance gate and which was the exit gate? So that the men were posted at the right gate.

For this purpose, signs with appropriate markings were to be fixed. They would thus honor the name of their town, after all, they were in Schilda.

Anyone traveling to Schilda today and leaving the town will notice two men turned to stone on the town gate, holding a large cloth in their hands and still waiting for the nocturnal intruder. They did not die of hunger, but of waiting, and serve as a monument in stone reminding us that no nocturnal intruder can secretly leave the city, at least in theory, because how can two figures turned to stone prevent sinister figures from leaving this strange place at night?

9.
Crap remains crap, what crap!

*I*t was a great day for Schilda. Everyone who had rendered outstanding services to the tranquil little town was honored in public on the festively decorated market square, where they were presented with a coin specially minted for them. The event took an unforeseen course when a coin of honor fell from the mayor's hand at the very moment when the town's most sensitive resident was to be honored.

It is no longer possible to say what his merit was. The misfortune was not that the coin fell, but where it fell. The person to be honored insisted that a fly had just been sitting where the coin now lay, and for a conspicuously long time, which could only mean that it had been doing its business in this place, that it was now stuck to the coin and that he was not willing to have such an ornate medal tied around him.

Nor could he be persuaded to touch the coin, put it under the magnifying glass of his sharp gaze and thus prove his bold assertion. Instead, he managed to persuade the mayor to hold the coin under his nose. And indeed, it exuded a strange smell that could have been a thousand times more potent than a cesspool. That alone was enough to justify the honoring of the person in question, even in retrospect, because of his precise powers of observation and even more meticulous conclusions.

The mayor was still lost in thought as to how to deal with the situation when a veritable shower of money poured down on him, and in a short time he thought he was sinking under a mountain of money. Suddenly no-one was sure that their own money had not been sullied in the same way, everyone wanted to get rid of their money as quickly as possible, mind you, the money and not the mayor. It was more a matter of chance that the rain of money – for the same reason, it's impossible to talk of a windfall – fell in the direction of the mayor.

Needless to say, no thief could be persuaded to go about his work for some time, as he would have had to touch the money, which even a thief could not be expected to do. The citizens of

Schilda had thus discovered that money stinks and, incidentally, was also the cause of this evil. However, this did not solve the problem. All the money was in the hands of the state in the form of a pile above the mayor and as no-one wanted to own any more money until this situation was resolved, public life was in danger of collapsing.

A meeting of the brightest minds was convened to solve the problem.

One woman explained that the easiest thing to do was to scrub the coins properly. There were plenty of brushes, apart from toothbrushes for a start, and then anyone could safely handle them again.

As luck would have it, even the most scrupulous and, for well-known reasons, not yet honored citizen was part of this council meeting.

He argued that you only had to bear in mind the size of the fly speck and the distance between the brush hairs. It wouldn't be enough to brush over the coin a thousand times in the hope of accidentally catching and brushing away the fly muck. He also called for a solution that would eliminate all flies at the same time so that similar incidents would not occur in the future.

A heated argument arose between the woman and the fussy citizen, which was only settled when the former village policeman spoke.

Certainly, one had to think about the time afterwards, which meant nothing other than returning the coins to their original owners. Brushing would destroy all traces, fingerprints, personal skin and sweat residue and the like, making it impossible to assign them later.

That made sense to everyone. Although no-one wanted to have anything to do with the money at the moment, most of them were burning inside to hold their money in their hands as quickly as possible, hopefully after it had been thoroughly cleaned and no longer stank.

Now he knew, the old policeman continued, that a poison had to be treated with an antidote. He could not say whether the antidote was fly dung, but he could well imagine that every coin would soon shine in perfect purity if it were placed in the blossom of a flower for a suitable period of time. Flowers are the epitome of purity and, incidentally, the money would not only no longer stink, but would smell of roses, hyacinths and all sorts of other things. A specific scent could even be provided for certain circles, so that in future money could no longer be recognized by its size and the superfluous numbers painted on it, but simply by the different scents.

This proposal was immediately accepted. All that was needed now were brave souls who were prepared to touch the coins disfigured with fly dung and soon all the coins were placed in the various blossoms of the flowers. As soon as this was done, the flowers closed tighter than a locker and unfortunately could no longer be persuaded to open.

From then on, the citizens of Schilda still indeed had money, but they could no longer get their hands on it, as is the way of life. In addition, the flowers were no longer graceful to look at, as they tensely kept their blossoms closed so as not to give up their precious treasure.

The honorable citizen, whose well-deserved tribute had failed because of his meticulous precision due to a tiny speck of fly dung, was nevertheless satisfied, as he did not have to carry around a lifetime of unnecessary weight because of the missed tribute that he wanted to hang around his neck, when his neck was meant

to carry his head around and not chains, pearls,
silver coins and other stuff.

10.

A strange and unfortunate chain of events

When the ceiling threatened to fall on Uhlenspiegel's head once again, and he was living in a cathedral-like old dilapidated castle with very high ceilings at the time, he decided to make his way to Schilda once again. Important changes needed to be discussed and introduced, a small flood of mental lightning had coursed through his brain last night, now the citizens of Schilda were to benefit from his suffering, because suffering is undoubtedly what it means when lightning, even if it is only mental, passes through a soft structure like the human brain and leaves strange traces.

He spent the journey in a pleasant mood and reached the peaceful town two days later. When the citizens of Schilda saw him from afar, they gathered like good children – or should we say lambs, as they were already used to Uhlenspiegel calling them together at the market, as he had once again appeared to tell them something important.

You citizens of Schilda, Uhlenspiegel began, you are the most intelligent people I have ever met from one end of the scale.

However, he did not specify from which side the observer's yardstick was set up.

But what a miserable life you lead as you imprison yourselves. As if you were dangerous predators, you lock yourselves in your houses, barred doors and windows, so that you can sleep peacefully at night, if you can't stay awake. Why this self-chastisement? cried Uhlenspiegel, By what right do you lock yourselves up, and your wives, children, dogs, cats, fleas and whatever else creeps and flies in your houses?

The robbers, some answered timidly, slowly realizing their guilt. We don't shut ourselves in, we shut the robbers out.

How on earth can the spirit of the great world blow in and through your huts if you lock them up, Uhlenspiegel insisted. You are right about the robbers. And this evil must be remedied with the same evil.

The citizens of Schilda did not understand, so Uhlenspiegel had to elaborate:

Think of the animals in your forest, Uhlenspiegel continued. Each has its territory, the bear, the wolf, the lynx, where one is, no other dares to go. And don't the robbers also live in the forest? Well, then, once there is a robber you know in the forest, no-one else will dare to enter unless he knows you and you know what to expect. But I will offer my services to become a robber in your forest so that you are safe from the others.

That made sense. They could work out what to expect from Uhlenspiegel, it was not a little, though it was still better than not knowing what to expect.

A week passed, Uhlenspiegel lived as the robber of Schilda, and all the citizens thought they were safe. One by one, they left their doors open during the day or even at night and enjoyed the freedom they had gained, the breath of the wide world that blew into their homes and their heads through the open doors. Uhlenspiegel had expected more entertainment from all this. So, it came in handy that he knew a strange journeyman from earlier. He commissioned him to make a racket in Schilda the following night as a robber. And so it happened.

The next day, the citizens of Schilda were horrified that a strange rogue had ventured into their territory during the night, when it was already occupied by Uhlenspiegel. He turned himself in unsuspectingly. After thinking for a while, he said:

It can mean nothing other than that my reputation is not terrible enough. No other robber fears me, even the smallest scoundrel poaches in my territory and yours.

He almost began to cry, so that everyone was overcome with pity.

I must gain a formidable reputation as a robber and you must help me, suggested Uhlenspiegel, his voice choking with tears.

This also made sense, just as all of Uhlenspiegel's suggestions made sense and yet often led to disasters.

The mayor passed a law that allowed Uhlenspiegel to attack, rob and, if necessary, beat up a citizen of Schilda whenever he pleased. This would give Uhlenspiegel a terrible reputation and not even the most dangerous robber in the world would ever venture into Schilda again.

Uhlenspiegel made ample use of the law. Hiding behind the trees, he lay in wait for the citizens of Schilda and beat them to death with his wooden club. If he felt like it, he would appear on the market square in broad daylight and, in a rage, crush quite a few of the goods on sale. At night he would run into the houses like someone out for a Sunday morning stroll, plundering the pantries, jewelry from the drawers, gold coins from the savings stockings and, especially with the women, tearing off the covers so that they had to spend the rest of the night freezing.

After a week, Uhlenspiegel realized that robbing was truly exhausting work. While the others slept, he had to go about his robbery and undergo the strenuous task of hauling away all the heavy treasures. Soon there was no citizen of Schilda left who hadn't had at least one bone damaged or their skin turned into a blue-marbled landscape.

So that everyone could get an idea of his efforts, he allowed the citizens of Schilda to do the same and rob each other the following night. Not much resulted; Uhlenspiegel had already dragged most of it away. But the little that the townspeople managed to snatch from each other on that last disastrous night had to be carried home to Uhlenspiegel in a long nightly column.

Thus ended Uhlenspiegel's existence as a robber. The citizens of Schilda, however, had bought themselves the freedom to leave their houses open, day and night. For the next few years, no robbers dared to enter their town.

For fear of the terrible reputation of their territorial robber, the honorable citizens of Schilda thought. But the reason was different. Word had simply gotten around in the robbery trade that there was nothing left to get in Schilda. Uhlenspiegel had done an excellent job. He sat for a few more days in the land of milk and honey he had robbed instead of doing his duty in the forest of Schilda and thought about returning to Schilda in a few days as a quack doctor. There were enough broken bones to set and wounds to heal, enough to rob the citizens of the pitiful remnant of the nothing they had left. It would be a robbery, since nature knew best how to heal wounds and didn't need a quack, especially not if he was called Uhlenspiegel.

11.
Illusory painting

$\mathcal{T}$he next time Uhlenspiegel visited Schilda, he mysteriously carried an elongated object wrapped in gray linen under his arm. It was a time when people communicated intensively with each other, even though they had none of the means of communication that are indispensable today. Contrary to his usual habit, Uhlenspiegel made a big secret of the matter under his arm, dispensing with the usual loquacious communications and simply remaining silent. Lured by the secrecy, the citizens of Schilda soon followed him, just as the children had once followed the Pied Piper of Hamelin.

Why are you staring at me? Uhlenspiegel turned to the line behind him. I know myself that I am about to grow old and wrinkled. If I were a woman, life would probably turn me into a witch with its mischievous moods. But as it is, I'm sure I'll end up as a haggard Rumpelstiltskin one day.

He scowled at everyone, as if he wanted to turn every single citizen of Schilda standing around into a stone monster. However, when he realized that the citizens of Schilda were already on the hook of curiosity, his face brightened, and he turned the inside of the cloth towards the others. What emerged was the image of a youthful, heroic Uhlenspiegel, as if he had only eaten fruit and vegetables all his life, slept all day long and devoted the rest of his time to maintaining his appearance.

I'm getting old, said Uhlenspiegel, oblivion is taking possession of me, so that soon I won't even remember the prime of my life. This must be remedied. By always looking like the prime of my life. You can't forget what doesn't change. So I have to make sure that the flower does not wither. Hence this wondrous scarf. It is as wide and long as a silk sheet and as deep as a plaster cast. I bought it in the Far East, where everyone walks around covered in these scarves. This cloth presses itself on your miserable old body and, whether age wants it or not, imposes its youthful appearance on it. However, no-one can expect you to walk around in these cloths. It's not hot enough for that in your peaceful town, not like in the Far East.

Have no worries. Simply lay this scarf on yourself at night. Over time, your body will be adorned with the beautiful youthful image. And since it knows height and depth like a plaster cast, the miserable wrinkles will be pressed away at the same time. And if you press it firmly enough against you, not only will your body become smooth and shiny as before, but so will your wrinkled insides and creaking joints. But remember, since you are made up of a front part and a back part, you must turn yourselves over like a chicken on a spit halfway through the night.

How is this to be done? You will ask yourselves as you are asleep. How shall we turn over? At the right time and not too often. I tell you, for what other reason did you marry? See to it that one of you keeps watch half the night and turns the other during that time. Then do it the other way round. Everything will be in its proper order. How could you be happy if you walk along forever in your youthful bloom and your second half withers away as a Rumpelstiltskin or a witch.

The speech did not fail to have an effect. As Uhlenspiegel was also somewhat talented at painting, he soon had the citizens of Schilda immortalized on a considerable number of cloths. On this occasion, all the strange whims of nature, such as large, cucumber-shaped noses, donkey-like ears, triple-curved chins and the like, were rectified. This was also no problem for the wondrous cloths.

This masterful art came at a reasonable price. Each one cost three quarters of the buyer's fortune. So Uhlenspiegel demanded the same amount of everything in proportion to their savings and considered it his fairness. He explained this to the poor.

To the rich, however, he explained that he had spent an infinitely greater amount of skill and time on them to create their perfect image. After all, they were certainly of a nobler nature than the common servants and deserved a more appropriate appearance that visibly set them apart from the others.

After a short time, every citizen of Schilda was equipped with this scarf. It is easy to imagine how the nights went from then on, because soon afterwards it seemed as if Father Stork had decided not to bring any more children to Schilda. It could have been for no other reason than that nobody wanted to sacrifice even a second of their precious night time to take off the cloth in order to assist Father Stork, as the cloth lost the time to do its work to perfection.

Once everyone had been taken care of, Uhlenspiegel had to expand his activities to other fields. And he did indeed extend it to fields. Soon the cows were standing in the meadow wrapped in wondrous blue and purple cloths, with udders the size of which no-one had ever seen before painted on the lower edge.

Even some trees and rose bushes were swathed in shiny golden cloths. And finally, the cloth craze took hold of the children, who were only sparingly brought by Father Stork; they were wrapped in cloths bearing the likeness of Nefertiti or a heroic Greek god.

Now that the property of the citizens of Schilda had been collected to such an extent and success was not yet apparent on the expectant faces, Uhlenspiegel thought it advisable to retire for a well-earned break. Before that, the citizens of Schilda had to be kept busy for the time being. A busy activity might distract them from the unfortunate undertaking and make them forget it.

Citizens of Schilda, Uhlenspiegel began his last speech on the market square. Success has not quite come yet. I have racked my brains a lot over this. And here lies the root of all evil, in your heads. Your minds are still occupied with too many useless tasks for your bodies to have enough time to take in the beautiful picture on the cloths. You must unburden your minds. Look around this market square. Here stands the town hall, here the inn, here the tailor's house, here the shoemaker's house. Why should each of you remember all these different things? Each of you just keep one thing in your head. If he then stands like an ox at the barn door in front of a building he doesn't know, he simply asks the person who does.

The citizens of Schilda did not understand him and Uhlenspiegel felt compelled to be clearer.

Take the multiplication table, why do you want to stuff your heads with all that? One person remembers how much is one and one. The second memorizes how much one and two is. The third, on the other hand, teaches his head the result if you put one together with three. If the first person, who only knows how much one and one is, needs to know how much one and two is, then he simply goes to his neighbor and asks him.

Now it could happen that his neighbor has just remembered something else. Where do you see the problem? Just go to the next neighbor and so on until you have found the one who has remembered how much one and two is. How many wonderful conversations you can then look back on until you realize the result.

Do the same with all things, with the names of your children as well as the names of trees and animals. Soon your head will be wonderfully free, and your bodily shell will find enough leisure to take on the young masquerade on your cloths, so that soon only young heroes will float through your tranquil place.

How it all ended is not known. Only that after a while, Father Stork started bringing new children to Schilda again. How else could it be that the citizens of Schilda can still be found on earth today and not just in a few places?

12.

Unique(ly) topsy-turvy Christmas world

*I*t so happened that Christmas was once again preparing to descend on the land of the Schilda citizens. The last few years had been bleak, marked by hardship and sorrow, withered fields and emaciated cattle. And Christmas was a reflection of these barren times. So Uhlenspiegel decided to put an end to all this misery himself.

You have to turn time upside down, he thought, then everything will turn upside down, so to speak, and the misery would turn into a wondrous sound (Ton = sound-> <-Not = misery), the O could remain in the middle, could even turn itself upside down without changing its egg-shaped appearance, but the first and last letters of Not (misery) had to be reversed.

As it was still early in the Advent season, it wasn't a good idea to get dressed up in the hot Santa costume just yet. Besides, it was time to start turning things upside down. Uhlenspiegel picked up a red apple, the color of which was incredibly similar to that of Santa Claus and turned it upside down to see which color came out if someone turned the apple upside down.

The winter sun shone wonderfully through the window and the apple was clothed in a warm mixture of blue and green. The colors had been decided. The white beard turned upside down made a pointed hat and the boots turned upside down simply made nothing where the feet belonged. Which meant that he had to stomp barefoot through the snow as a blue-green Santa Claus with a pointed black hat on his head. The citizens of Schilda were quite astonished when this strange apparition came to their town. For Uhlenspiegel, there was no time to lose, good works cannot be delayed.

Citizens of Schilda, he said, you look at me and are certainly wondering who sent me. For this much is clear, if I come to you, someone must have sent me, what else – and Uhlenspiegel spoke the following part of his speech in a strange mumble – can move a refined spirit like me to visit your gloomy village. Knecht Ruprecht (Santa Claus's assistant who punishes bad children) himself has sent me personally to lay out the path for him, so to speak, and to prepare everything for his arrival. And what a glorious arrival it will be. Gone will be the evenings of miserable hardship, the adversity, the worries. Everything will shine in gold, silver and purple, the tables will buckle under the weight of the most delicious food and the Christmas trees will glow as if all the stars of heaven were hanging from them.

We'll turn everything upside down, continued Uhlenspiegel, we'll turn misery on its head. The result will be the most glorious feast, which will remain engraved in your wooden minds as a revered memory.

He said the last part again in that strange mumbling tone.

We are about to begin the Advent season. What a waste of joy to light just one candle at first. If you can be happy with one candle, how much more with four. So light all four candles on the first Sunday of Advent and rejoice in the glorious light. Just leave the candles burning and do nothing else but light the second burning candle again the next Sunday of Advent. Have you ever had the experience of lighting a lighted candle a second time? It will then shine for you with two flames. We will continue in this way until each of the four candles is lit with four flames.

This made sense and the citizens of Schilda ran into their homes to turn the Advent season upside down.

The next day, Uhlenspiegel told the citizens of Schilda to decorate a Christmas tree with the rest of the treasures that misery had left them. This was also done, and soon the Christmas trees were hung with strings of beads, old golden rings, coins on strings and the like.

Uhlenspiegel, meanwhile, ran to the mayor to suggest a Christmas service.

The time has come, Uhlenspiegel began to make his proposal, to spruce up Schilda. And doesn't that first mean picking up all the dirt from the streets? I myself will do my best to pick up all the dirt. But how can I pick it up if it doesn't belong to me? So first make a law that everything lying in the street is only my property.

What a strange fellow, thought the mayor, who even desires the dirt in the street. However, the suggestion sounded like a good idea and so the mayor issued the desired decree.

Christmas was fast approaching, and it was time to prepare the Christmas roast.

Look at your dogs, said Uhlenspiegel. Aren't they many times faster than your legs, and on top of that, they can detect all those wonderful smells that roam around at Christmas time a thousand times better. And their incomparable courage. After all, the strongest of them fight against bears and while you miserable creatures crawl despondently into your homes, these beasts appear.

Where do you think all this comes from? It is nothing other than the result of their Christmas feast that they are allowed to feast on the delicious bones of your roast goose. Therefore, proceed in the reverse way. Cut out the useless spicy crust, the juicy soft meat and give it to me. I will feed it to your dogs. But you are to feast on the delicious bones, so that you grow smelling noses on your faces, to enjoy the roast goose not only with your palate, but to see its wonderful smells, which are a thousand times more valuable, with your eyes and to devour them with your nose.

That also made sense. Only Uhlenspiegel didn't think to let the poor dogs share in the roast goose and ate no less than 50 crispy golden-brown goose breasts in a week.

Now Christmas Eve was just around the corner, time for presents, at least an evening that was all the wrong way round.

Why do you lock the Christmas trees in your little parlors, Uhlenspiegel railed. Aren't they used to the freedom of the forest, the air, the wind, frost, snow and ice? Put them outside your door and tomorrow I will walk through the streets to see the miracle of Christmas with my own eyes. Which means that this time we are turning the misery of previous years upside down, transforming it into a glamorous celebration.

This is how it happened. The citizens of Schilda stood in front of their houses, Christmas trees at their sides, and Uhlenspiegel marched through the alleyways as if he were taking part in a parade. At each tree, however, he paused briefly and told its owner to turn it upside down. In front of the stunned eyes of the Schilda citizens, Uhlenspiegel then collected all the treasures that fell from the trees as if a Christmas deluge was descending on Schilda.

The treasures lay in the street, and they belonged to Uhlenspiegel, so to speak. But isn't it the case that anyone who does something to help the plight of his fellow citizens during the festive Christmas season is entitled to a rich reward, which falls down on him from above, as it were, from the heavenly Christmas air, like the glittering gold coins that once fell on the little girl of the star.

La rue, c'est moi!, shouted Uhlenspiegel in a historical fit of madness and undauntedly picked up the treasure lying on the ground, which in a way represented the first road toll in history, and stowed it away in a state sack turned into a Christmas sack and in his bulging trouser pockets.

The citizens of Schilda, even if they wanted to stop the foolhardy man's audacity, were powerless. How could they stop him, since they had to hold on to their Christmas trees, which were standing on their tops, to prevent them from falling over. And a fallen Christmas tree was considered the worst omen that could befall anyone. Instead of bemoaning their fate, they should be grateful to Uhlenspiegel. In one fell swoop, he relieved them of all the worries associated with choosing the right Christmas presents.

Such worries are not insignificant, they easily overshadow the stresses and strains of a whole year. In the end, the citizens of Schilda themselves became the image of their Christmas trees. While they remained motionless at the side of their upside-down trees, an infinite number of white flakes fell down on them, beautiful ice crystals grew on them and at night the golden stars of the Christmas sky clung to their frozen limbs.

Index

Biography

After graduating from high school in Berlin, I studied medicine in Berlin and Munich and worked in medicine for around 40 years after my studies. I have been retired since the end of 2022. During my professional career I also wrote some manuscripts, a book for young people, children's books, novels and poems. Some have since been self-published.

In addition the author has published several
novels in English translation:

Manu's Journey With Death
- A fugue through time
A life, narrated on several levels, accompanied in its
tracks and followed by death. In
some places, points of this life that have long since
passed light up, a brief glowing
breath where it pauses for a moment before it is
dragged on by the stream of life and
disappears somewhere, not without trace but forever.
What remains? In any case,
death, even if no one is interested in the remnants of
this trace of life.

Chrystillian Christmas –
Christmas as usual ~~and~~ different
A goose on its flight to baking-oven land, chasing a
golden angel's curl, encountering a mutant Christmas
tree, an endless line of waiting stars, Santa's great-
great-ancestor and, of course, Father Christmas
himself, sitting on a cloud under whose shadow a boy is
riding down from the peaks of the Andes, spreading the
news of Christ's birth ... It could be like that, but it isn't
quite, maybe a little, but just maybe. An Advent
calendar of Christmas short stories, profound and
loving, varied and multi-faceted, presented in a
wonderful narrative style that will enchant even the
adult reader. A fragrance-wrapped Christmas soufflé

that can be eaten over 26+1 days, on each day of Advent and Christmas plus New Year's Eve, or all at once, depending on the size of your appetite or Christmas taste ...

The Island of Figures
Youth Novel

A little girl in Japan receives a doll from her father for her birthday. When the girl is older, the doll is placed on the waves of the sea in a small boat. Apparently a tradition to mark the transition to a new phase of life into adulthood.

Some time later, another girl travels after her missing doll, and an exciting, adventurous journey begins with an unusual, surprising end.

Allegories
Short Stories Volume 1 -4

The following collection in 4 volumes contains just over 60 short stories, each short story is based on a biblical passage from the New Testament like a parable and is applied to our time. A short time to catch your breath, a short time perhaps to reflect, a short time perhaps to delve deeper. Although Christ used everyday life for his parables, they still leave a deep impression today. They are easy to remember with a hidden important message that we discover when we think about them.

Roxanna
And the Mysterious Monk

Detective Roxanna has solved her first case when life, or rather death, puts another case on her desk. This brings her into contact with a wealthy English gentleman at his country estate, who has amassed a considerable fortune with an unusual business idea. Among them is a complicated hunter, who is not only a little over-the-top in his language, and especially a monk who, with his incredible intuition, not only beats the inspector to it once.

Roxanna
The Fatal Secret of the Murder Books

It begins with a murder, a somewhat bizarre female detective, events that take place in Rome, England and France. A story that jumps back to the Middle Ages, runs on two tracks, two suspicious women and a dead man who suddenly appears one night to one of the two suspects. A tangled criminal string that seems to have been partially untangled by diligent endeavours — only to become even more tangled in the next moment and finally, seemingly lying in front of you untangled in a perfectly straight line.

Uhlenspiegel with the Schilda Citizens
Volume 1 - 3

Uhlenspiegel, the lone warrior, armed with an army of mischievous thoughts, encounters a village full of Schilda citizens who are less armed, or rather, armed with different thoughts. Uhlenspiegel's premise: "Where money is at stake, it's good to be good!" And so he mischievously plays out his insights on the Schilda citizens who, with their naive way of thinking, are the appropriate antagonists. Does such an encounter make sense? Amusing and entertaining, in any case!